OLD MACDONALD
DRIVES A TRACTOR

DON CARTER

ROARING BROOK PRESS
NEW MILFORD, CONNECTICUT

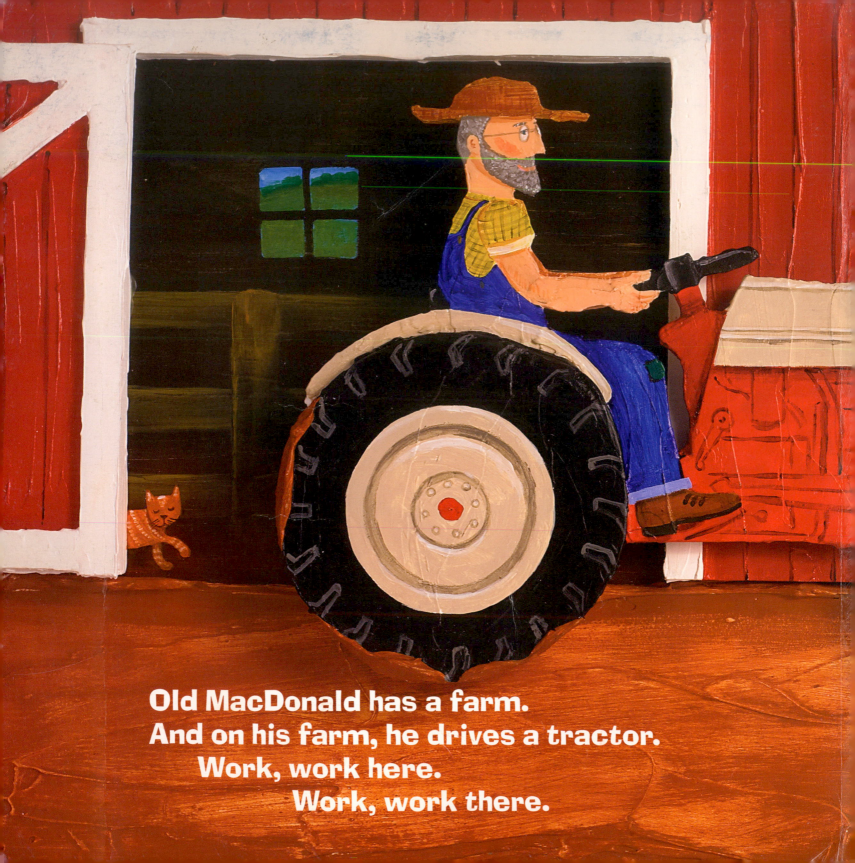

Old MacDonald has a farm.
And on his farm, he drives a tractor.
Work, work here.
Work, work there.

That old tractor works just about everywhere!

Old MacDonald drives a tractor.
And on that tractor, he pulls a plow.
Plow, plow here.
Plow, plow there.

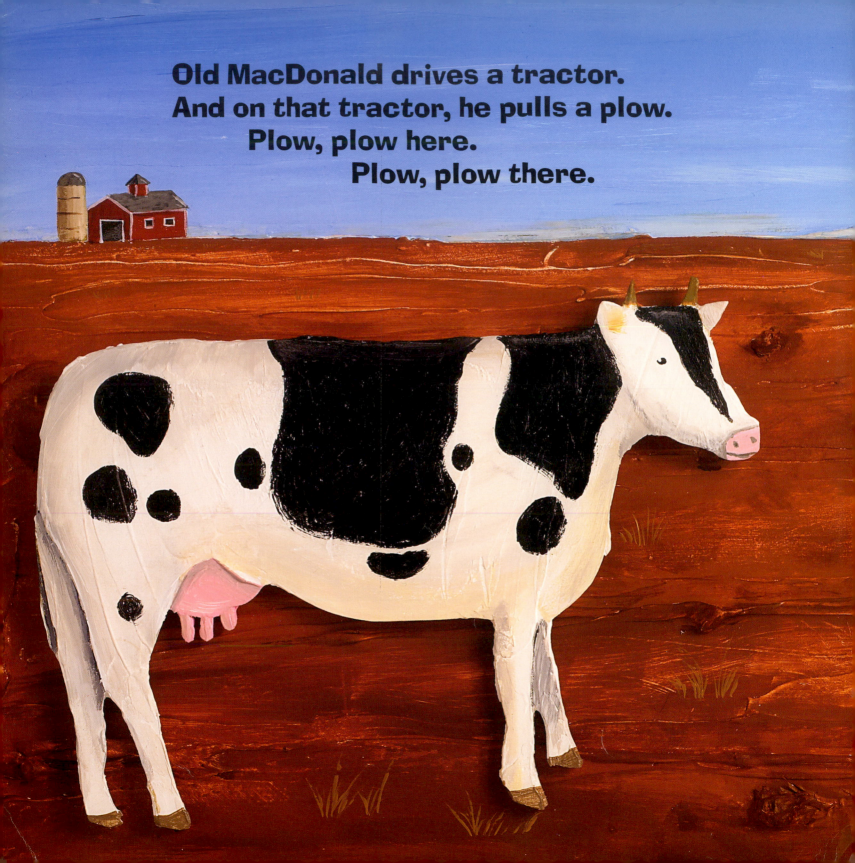

Plow until that field is clear!

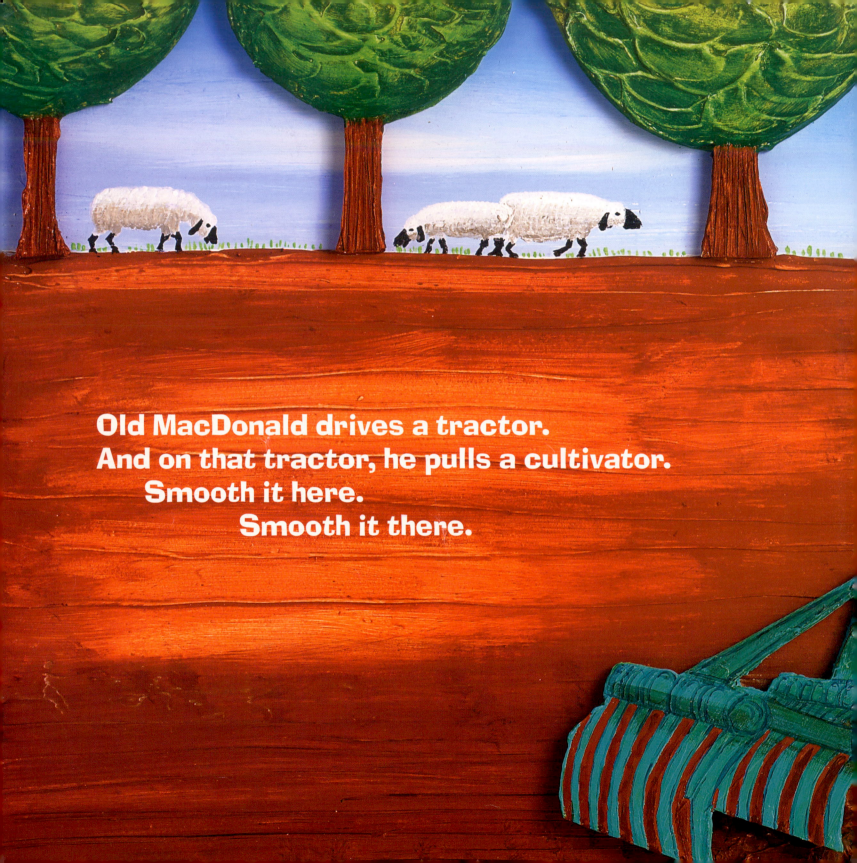

Old MacDonald drives a tractor.
And on that tractor, he pulls a cultivator.
Smooth it here.
Smooth it there.

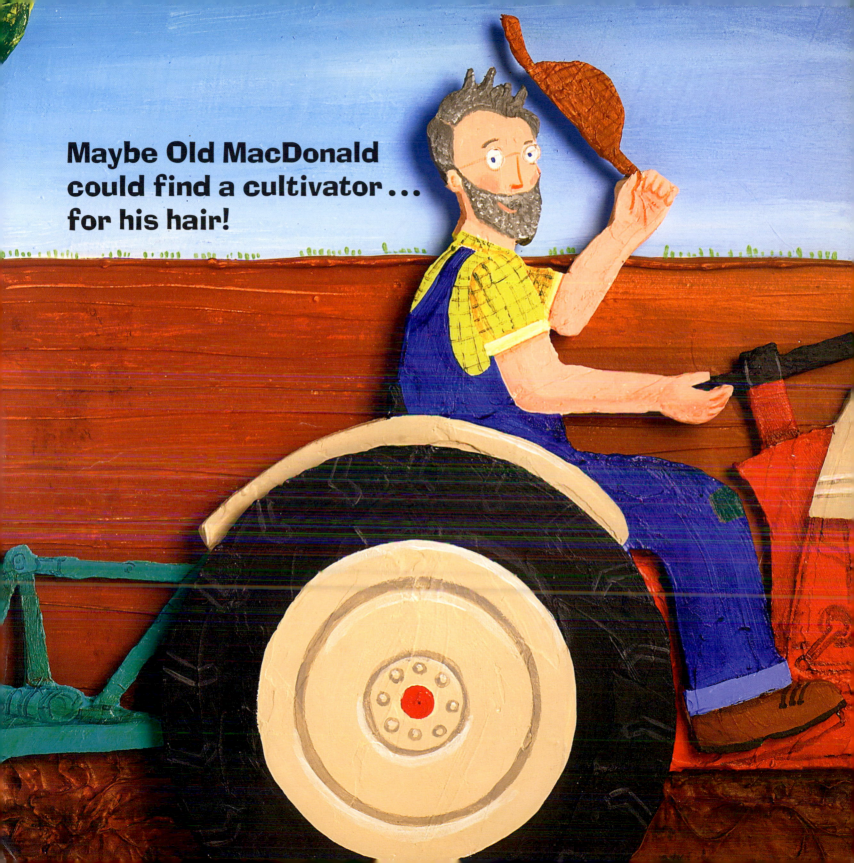

Maybe **Old MacDonald** could find a cultivator... for his hair!

Old MacDonald drives a tractor.
And on that tractor,
he pulls a seed drill.
Pfffft, pfffft here.
Pfffft, pfffft there.

Spitting seeds into holes with blasts of air!

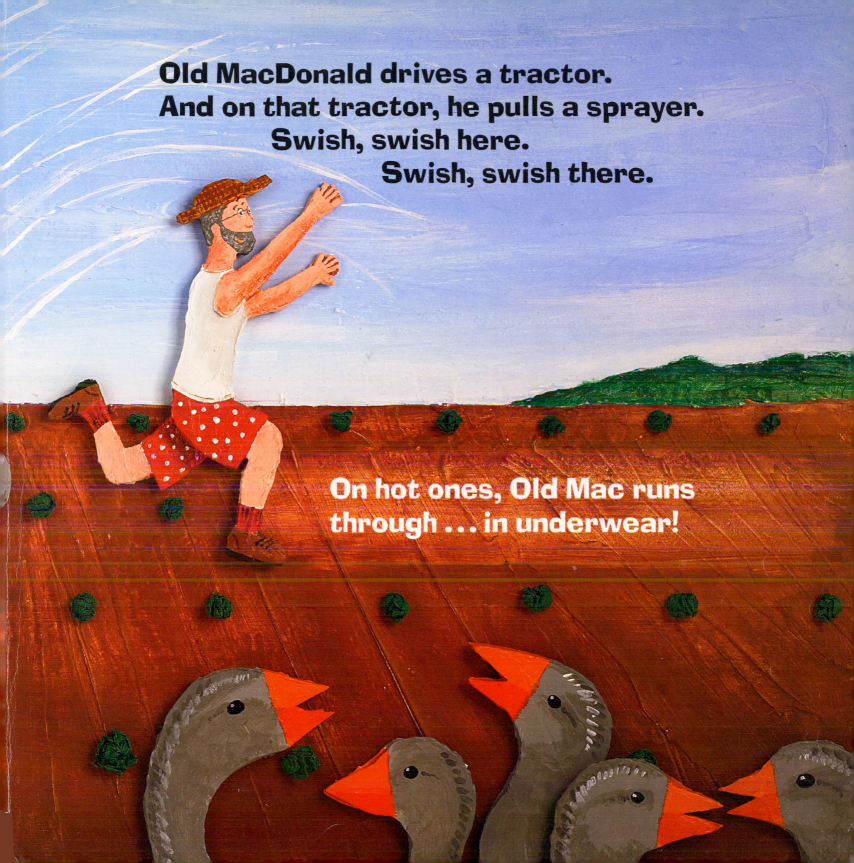

Old MacDonald drives a tractor.
And on that tractor, he pulls a sprayer.
Swish, swish here.
Swish, swish there.

On hot ones, Old Mac runs
through . . . in underwear!

Old MacDonald drives a tractor.
And on that tractor, he follows a combine.
Cut, cut here.
Cut, cut there.

Cut his wheat field down to bare!

Old MacDonald drives a tractor.
And on that tractor, he pulls a spreader.
Manure here.

Manure there.

You can smell it all the way . . .
to Delaware!

Old MacDonald drives a tractor.
And on that tractor, he pulls a harvester.
Pull one here.

Pull one there.

Mac pulls carrots the easy way — in a chair!

Old MacDonald drives a tractor.
And on that tractor, he pulls a baler.
A roll of hay here.
A roll of hay there.

Hungry horses stop and stare.

Old MacDonald drives a tractor.
And on that tractor, he pulls a flatbed.

Oink,
oink
here.

Old MacDonald drives a tractor.
And on that tractor, he worked all day.
Yawn, yawn here.
Yawn, yawn there.

**Old MacDonald
climbs the stair.**

To Ronnie Wade and the farmers of America past, present and future

Published by Roaring Brook Press
Roaring Brook Press is a division of
Holtzbrinck Publishing Holdings Limited Partnership
143 West Street, New Milford, Connecticut 06776

Distributed in Canada by H.B. Fenn and Company Ltd.
Book Design by Tania Garcia

Library of Congress Cataloging-in-Publication Data
Carter, Don, 1958-
  Old MacDonald drives a tractor / Don Carter.
       p. cm.
  Summary: Old MacDonald and his tractor can handle most
of the work on the farm, from pulling a plow, to following a
combine, to going home at night, in a rhyming tale reminiscent
of the children's song, Old MacDonald had a farm.
  ISBN-13: 978-1-59643-023-5
  ISBN-10: 1-59643-023-0
  [1. Tractors--Fiction. 2. Farm life--Fiction. 3. Stories in rhyme.]
I. Title.
  PZ8.3.C2445Old 2007
  [E]--dc22
                                        2006014273

Roaring Brook Press books are available
for special promotions and premiums.
For details contact:
Director of Special Markets, Holtzbrinck Publishers.

Printed in China

First Edition June 2007

2 4 6 8 10 9 7 5 3 1